T0149515

Inside Lily's World

by
Susan Horton

authorHOUSE®

AuthorHouse™
1663 Liberty Drive
Bloomington, IN 47403
www.authorhouse.com
Phone: 1-800-839-8640

Published by AuthorHouse   10/26/12

ISBN: 978-1-4772-7627-3 (sc)
ISBN: 978-1-4772-7626-6 (e)

Library of Congress Control Number: 2012918560

Contents

Chapter 1
The Big Move

A moving truck pulled up to the porch of Lillian Thompson's grandmother's house. Since her father got a new promotion at work, the family had to leave the peaceful surroundings of the country and take on the hustle and bustle of the big city. Two tall, husky men in jumpsuits began loading the boxes from the porch into the trailer of the truck.

"Mom, can I take my bicycle with me?" This

was Lily's first move so she was not sure how to pack.

"Sure! You can bring along anything that will fit in those two suitcases and that box." She said with a smile.

"Oh mom." Lily knew her mother was joking, but she was a bit disappointed that she would have to leave most of her toys behind.

"I'm sorry sweetie, but there is just not enough room to bring everything with us on this move, but as soon as we get settled in the city and get a bigger place, you can bring everything home." She sat on Lily's bed and gave her a hug. Just then her grandmother walks in and joins them.

"I promise sweetheart, I will leave your room just as you left it....only neater!" She began to tickle Lily.

This made Lily feel better about leaving her friends, her school, and her home. It's not easy to pick up and go away from everything you have ever known. Her mother told her that it was a good move and that it will help her father move ahead in the workplace.

Just then Lily's grandfather comes in the room wearing a sombrero. He began to dance and snap his fingers. Lily loved it when Papito entertained. That was the best part of having so many different heritages, there was always something fun to do. One thing was for certain, she knew that she was going to miss her family.

Sensing her sadness, her grandmother said, "I know! Let's have a party and celebrate our little papoose!" Lily's grandmother was Native American and she loved the ritual of celebration. For instance on Lily's birthdays she made dishes from all of the cultures that made up this very diverse family. Her mother's father was from Mexico. Her mother's mother was a member of the Alabama-Coushatta tribe of Texas. On Lily's father's side her grandmother was Filipino and his father was African-American. Just about every race was represented and accounted for in the Thompson's house.

Lily's grandmother quickly climbed the stairs to the attic and began rummaging thru that old trunk. She was looking for all the decorations she had tucked away for the various holidays. She hangs up a bunch of balloons, a piñata she filled with candies and toys, and lots of colorful lanterns. She also filled a basket with mangoes, star fruit, plums, kiwi and lit candles to complete the table decorations.

Papito brought in his cal do tlalpeno, which was a chicken and vegetable soup made with rice, chopped avocado, white cheese and chipotle chile pepper. Then Momu placed her famous fried rabbit beside that. The rest of Lily's family began to arrive and the table began to get crowded with different delicacies. For instance, Reyna, her father's mother, brought her crispy pata, which is deep fried pig's leg. She also brought collard greens seasoned with smoked turkey necks and salt water cornbread to represent the African-American community. The feast of cultures being complete, the family all joined hands and began to offer thanks for their fellowship and love in all the different languages.

Chapter 2
Lily's New School

The Thompson family move was a great success.

Lillian loved her new neighborhood, and she was happy about that she got her own room, but she was very nervous about her new school.

"Momma, why do I have to change schools?" She asked her mother who was very excited too.

"Lily we have talked about this before. Your old school is too far of a commute and your father and I would both be late for work. Your new school may be fun.

Disappointed, Lily went to her room and began to look thru her photo album. She missed all her friends and her old school already. She didn't know what to expect from the new people in her life. What if they didn't like her? What if she didn't fit in? What if she wouldn't like them?

The next day when she awoke and began getting dressed for school, Lily cried. She was so nervous about the new school until she couldn't finish her breakfast.

Sensing Lily's pain, her mother put her arms around her and began to comfort her.

"It will be better than you expect sweetie." Lily's mom wanted to put her mind at ease.

As she walked Lily out to the bus stop, Ms Thompson gave her another hug and said, "Baby girl I will be right here when you get home this afternoon. Have a great day and remember I love you." With that being said, the bus pulls up and Lily's mother gave her a peck on the cheek and helped her with her book bag. As Lily took her seat next to a thin girl with strawberry blonde hair and freckles, she waved one last goodbye to her mommy.

"Hi, my name is Mary. You must be the new girl." She gave Lily a smile.

Feeling better Lily responded, "Yes. My name is Lily."

"Ms Collins told us we were getting a new classmate yesterday. Where did you move from?"

As Lily began to chat with Mary about her family and where they came from she forgot all about her nervousness. They had such a great conversation Lily almost forgot they were on their way to school. When they arrived, Mary gave Lily a small tour and told her where the cafeteria, the gym, and the school supply store was and then she introduced her to Ms. Collins.

"Welcome Lily! We are so happy to have you here. Let me show you to your desk." Ms Collins was a beautiful young lady with a smile that brightened up the room. Lily felt so much better knowing that everyone was so warm and welcoming. She could hardly wait to meet the rest of her class.

"Good morning class." Ms Collins was very pleasant.

"Good morning Ms Collins!" The class all chimed in at once.

"Today we will be starting a new chapter in our readers. Please take them from underneath your desks and open them to page 14." Everyone did as they were instructed, except Lily.

"Ms Collins, I don't have a book yet." Lily's mother had not had a chance to fill her school supply list yet, because of the move and some of the materials were still on back order at the school supply store.

"Who will be kind enough to share with Lily?" Three people raised their hands. One of them was Mary, her new friend from the bus. The next was a little African-American girl name Leticia and the other was a Caucasian boy, with blonde hair, by the name of Peter.

"Leticia, since you are closest to Lily, why don't you slide your desk over so that she can see." Before she could finish her sentence, Leticia did just that. She opened to page 14 and pointed to the beginning paragraph. Just then Ms Allred, the school secretary called over the intercom.

"Ms Collins, please report to the office." The class started to make noises implying that Ms. Collins was in trouble.

The beautiful, enthusiastic teacher smiled shook her head and stood to exit the classroom. "Now don't get too loud. I will be right back."

"Ewww...you got to share a book with *Puke-ticia*!" Peter was being cruel for no reason. Leticia dropped her head in shame and shed a few tears.

Lily looked at Peter and asked, "Hey Peter, Peter *booger-eater*, you want to mind your own business!" This made everyone in the class laugh out loud; even Leticia. Peter began to turn beet red. He was totally embarrassed.

"You can make fun of me all you want but I

ain't got to share no book with a nigger!" This comment made everyone in the classroom become tense. Lily was hurt by this comment. She was part African-American and she was taught that people who use this word were trying to be mean and thought they were better than others.

"Class what is going on?" Ms Collins stormed back in and took her place behind the desk. "Just what happened when I left?"

Lily was the first to speak up. She always felt it was her place to be the voice of calm when things like this happened.

"Ms Collins Peter was making fun of Leticia's name so I tried to defend her. Then he turned really mean and said the "N" word." Lily folded her arms as if to take a stand against what Peter had done.

"Peter...do you have anything you want to say to Leticia and the rest of the class?" Ms Collins walked over to stand beside his desk. She put her hand on his shoulder and cleared her throat. "Peter...we are waiting."

Peter reluctantly mumbled a weak, "I'm

sorry." Then proceeded to explain "Well that's what my father calls black people! He has a name for all others too. He calls Chinese people *Chinks* and Hispanics *Spics*."

"Peter, just because someone else says something does not make it right. All people should be respected no matter what their race, gender, or religion. I'm sorry to tell you this sweetie, but your father is wrong. Do you honestly hate Leticia?" she asked.

"No ma'aam. I don't hate her, but my father says that I have to because they are what is wrong with our country. He says that all black people are lazy and that if they would get jobs they wouldn't be stealing money from him in taxes." Peter felt better knowing he had told them the truth.

Ms Collins walked her desk and took her seat. "Peter that rumor was an awful lie that was started by people who wanted to justify their hate for African-Americans. I happen to know that both Leticia's parents work and make large contributions to the less fortunate. They are good people and don't deserve to be put down for something that they didn't do. Do you think it is fair if I judged you based on something that someone else said you did that you didn't do?"

"No. I guess I would feel bad. I'm sorry Leticia." Peter apologized for real this time. Leticia gave him a forgiving smile.

"Class, please remember what the golden rule says. Who can tell me what that is?" Ms Collins asked. The entire class raised their hands. "Wow! Well since everyone here knows the answer, let us all say it together."

In unison, the entire class said in a sing-song way:

"Do unto others as you would have them do unto you."

Chapter 3
Lily Fights Back

Brent that's not fair!" Lily yelled.

Brent Dyson was the school bully and he had taken Lily's lunch money for the third time that week. She went home hungry the other two days because Brent threatened that if she told, he would beat her up.

Lily had never been beaten up by a boy before. Her mother and father always told her that fighting was wrong. So she sat and tried to figure a way to stop Brent from taking her lunch money.

The next day at school, Brent walked over to Lily and held out his hand.

"Cough up the dough!" Brent held out his hand expecting.

"No." Lily was determined not to let him win this time. After all, she wanted to eat lunch too. She got too hungry in the afternoons. "But I will share my food with you at lunch time." She said smiling.

"Nope, I don't want to share!" He held his hand out again.

"I'm sorry Brent but I will not give you my money." She stood her ground. No one should have the right to take from someone else. It's not fair and she was not going to stand for it.

Brent shrugged his shoulders and then pushed Lily to the ground. She fell knee first and her skirt flew up in the air. Bloodied and embarrassed, she began to cry. Everyone pointed and laughed at her. Lily didn't know what hurt worse her knee or her feelings.

As she picked herself up and began to dust off her skirt, Brent walks back over to her and demands her lunch money. Not wanting to be embarrassed again, she did as she was told.

"Now this is for making me wait." Brent pushed her down again. This time she landed face first. Her cheek was bruised and so was her pride. Lily sat in the dust and started to cry again. Not so much because she was in pain, but she was afraid. She didn't know what to do. She was afraid if she told her mother or father what has been happening, that Brent really would beat her up.

"Oh my God!" Lily's mother exclaimed as she walked in the door to their apartment.

When Lily heard her yell, she began to cry again herself. Her mother quickly took out the first aid kit and began to attend to the scratches and bruises. Lily felt better in her mother's care.

"Mom?" Lily was about to tell her what went wrong with Brent, but she remembered what he told her that he would do if she told on him.

"Yes sugar." Lily' mom looked at her with so much love and sympathy that she knew it would make her worry more if she said anything. So she decided to handle this on her own. She began to think of ways she could stop this bully from taking her lunch money and pushing her around.

The next day Lily got to the school yard a little earlier than usual because the traffic on 5th street was very light for some reason. When she walked across the yard she noticed that Brent was there with three other boys. One of the boys was bigger than Brent and it looked like he was taking his money. As she continued to watch in awe, she realized that is exactly what was going on. Then she saw the older boy push Brent down and kick dust on his clothes. The other boys who were watching began to laugh and point. Lily then heard the boy who was tormenting Brent say the same thing to him that he had said to her the day before. It all started to make sense. Brent was picking on her because someone was picking on him. Lily thought to herself if she could help him, maybe he would leave her alone. Brent told Lily not to tell anyone that he was bullying her. He didn't tell her that she could not tell if someone was bullying him.

At that moment Principal Green came over and put his hand on Lily's shoulder and said,"It's almost time for the bell."

"Mr. Green?" Lily was determined to make a difference.

"Yes Lily." He answered.

"What if I saw someone being bullied?" She was hoping he could help her.

"This school has a zero tolerance for such a thing. Whoever was bullying or participating any activity that caused harm to others would be expelled from school. Tell me, do you know of anything happening?" He was curious to know.

Lily began to fill Mr. Green in on what she had witnessed with Brent. She told him how the boys cornered him and took his money and began to make threats while pushing him around.

"Point them out to me!" Mr. Green was

outraged. He would not allow anyone to torment students on his watch. Lily did just that. He took out a small note pad and began to jot down all their names.

Later that day, Mr. Green called them all to the office, including Brent and Lily. He began the meeting with "Boys I hear that you have been bothering one of my students."

All of the older boys put on these angelic faces and shook their heads 'no'.

"Lily you want to tell these gentlemen what you saw?" Mr. Green pointed to Lily so that she could make it very clear what she witnessed.

Brent looked worried that she was going to tell on him. Lily was not there to help herself. She was there to help him. She figured that if she could rescue him, he would leave her alone. After all, a bully is someone who is in need of help. They were usually over weight or had hygiene problems or poor social skills. They felt the need to torture others to make themselves feel less inadequate. A bully is not someone to hate, but someone to pity.

"Well, in light of what Lily saw, I have no

choice but to suspend you all for 10 days. First, give Brent back his money and apologize for fighting him. Then I want you all to go see Ms. Allred for your suspension slips. You cannot return to school unless your parents come with you. Brent and Lily, you may return to class." Mr. Green gave Lily a wink that said thank you for coming forward.

Lily left out of the side door of the principal's office and Brent quickly followed. She was a bit frightened, what if he was angry that she told? She could have made things worse by trying to help him.

"Hey!" Brent tried to catch up to Lily who was now almost running.

"Hey kid!" He caught up to her and put his hand on her shoulder. "I just want to thank you for what you did." He then gave Lily back her money and ran down the hallway to his classroom.

Chapter 4
Lily Tells the Truth

Absolutely not!" Lily screamed. She and her best friend Mary were arguing to see who could jump with the rope the longest. After Lily made three attempts and only made it to 35, she began to feel a little jealous that Mary made it to 50 each time.

"Ok. We will try it again and this time whoever goes to 50 is the champion." Mary was very sure that it was going to be her. Lily was very competitive and did not like to lose, so she began to skip rope and only called out every other number. Mary was not a mean person and she saw that Lily was cheating so she didn't even take her turn.

"Lily I have to go." Mary was very disappointed in her friend. It was just a silly game. There was no need to cheat. Mary felt she didn't want to play with Lily anymore because of this.

"When are you coming back?" Lily asked confused. Mary did not answer. As a matter of fact she began to run so she did not have to answer any more questions.

Lily felt bad that Mary didn't want to play anymore so she went inside and told her mother. "Mom I don't think I want to play with Mary anymore."

Not sure what happened, her mother asked "Why is that sweetheart?"

"Well she cheats when we skip rope and I don't think that's fair." Lily knew that this was not true, but she could not stop herself from telling a lie. She didn't want to tell her mother that she and Mary had argued before about Lily cheating so she pretended it was Mary's fault to keep her mother on her side.

"Well sweetie, if Mary is a cheater then you don't want someone like that for a friend. I will just have to ask her mother not to allow Mary to come over anymore." This frightened Lily. What was she going to do without her best friend? Mary was the only one who reached out to her when she first moved to this area and they had been the best of friends every since. Was it so hard to tell the truth about what really happened? After all it was her fault. Mary wasn't the cheater she was, but how could she tell her mother that she just lied?

The next day on the bus Mary walked right by Lily who was seated in their usual seat. Mary waved a somber hello. It appeared that she was still angry about yesterday. Mary took a seat two windows away from Lily and began to stare in the other direction.

Lily tried to get Mary's attention so that she could apologize, but Mary was not paying attention. Her feelings were obviously hurt and there was nothing Lily could do to change that.

Later on that day it began to rain. Lily wanted to go over to Mary's house because this was the day that her mother would allow them to bake cookies or brownies as a rainy day activity. Because of the lie Lily told her mother about Mary, she could not go over to her best friend's house. Lily spent the rest of the afternoon in her room playing with her dolls and trying to read from one of her favorite books, The Adventures of Winnie the Pooh. Without Mary to read the lines for piglet and Tigger, it was no fun. She needed her best friend.

Mary began to wander throughout the apartment looking for something else to do when she saw the Faberge eggs her mother collected. She opened the china hutch where they were sitting and carefully picked up each one and inspected it. After she had placed the delicate treasures back in their place she closed the cabinet. When she pushed the door closed, one of the eggs began to topple, because it was not securely placed back on its holder. Lily tried to catch it before it fell and broke, but when she yanked on the hutch door, it fell and shattered completely. What was she going to do? Her mother told her specifically not to touch those eggs. Lily quickly swept up the pieces and hid them in the bottom of the china hutch. When the pieces where found and her mother asked what happened, Lily told a fib and said that the storm shook the apartment and knocked it off its holder. Lily's mother looked at her with a curious expression of her face. She took Lily's hand and led her to the kitchen table poured her a glass of milk and asked, "Dear are you familiar with the story of the boy who cried wolf?"

"No mama. Lily began to get excited, because her mother told the best stories and since it was raining, this would occupy her lonely day.

"Well, there was this little shepherd boy who was tending to his father's flock. Whenever his father came to check on him and the sheep, he would only ask if there had been any sightings of a wolf. The father was very concerned about this and wanted to protect his son and the herd. In order to stop the loss of any of the sheep the father asked his son to stay for extra shifts to make sure the sheep were protected. The son knew that the father cared for the sheep, but he grew very despondent and wanted to know if the father cared for him, so he decided to play a practical joke and yell, "THE WOLF! THE WOLF APPROACHETH!" Not only did his father come to his aid but several other farmers in the area came with their pitchforks and guns prepared to destroy this ravenous predator. When they arrived, they saw only the little shepherd boy. He was in no danger at all, so everyone returned to his home and bedded down for the night. Later on during the night the little boy got bored and decided he wanted some company so he began to cry once again, "THE WOLF! THE WOLF APPROACHETH!" And just as before, his father, the farmers even a few more town folk came to the little shepherd boy's aid. Also, just as before there was no wolf. This time the father warned him and said, "Son, be careful about crying "wolf" when you are not in trouble, for there may come a time when you need help and help is nowhere to be found." And then he along with all the others returned to their homes. The shepherd boy drifted off to sleep and was awakened by a loud growl. He saw that the wolf really was there and had taken his father's prize ewe for slaughter.

"THE WOLF! THE WOLF IS ATTACKING!" The little boy cried. This time no one came to help him. Not his father, not the other farmers, not even any of the other town's folk. The wolf got away with killing a sheep, because the little shepherd boy did not tell the truth.

Lily looked at her mother's kind face and dropped her head. She knew that her mother knew she had been lying about Mary and even about the collectable eggs.

"I'm sorry. I broke your eggs. I took them out of the china hutch to play with them and when I put it back, I didn't secure it." Lily reached for her mother's hand.

"I was the cheater; not Mary. I think I lost my best friend because I lied. I wish I could talk to her." Lily confessed.

"Well we can't fix the eggs, but I know what we can do to make it right with Mary." Lily's mother picked up the phone and dialed Mary's house and handed Lily the phone.

"Hello Ms. Wright, may I please speak to Mary?" Lily asked unsure of herself. What if Mary had told her mother about the cheating incident and didn't want Mary to be her friend anymore?

"Hello Lily! Where are you? Mary and I are making chocolate chip cookies and it's not the same without you. Are you coming over?" Mary's mother asked with enthusiasm.

"Sure! Let me ask my mother if it's ok." Lily looked at her mother who was already nodding her head yes.

When Lily walked into the front door she saw Mary in her favorite apron. She had chocolate on her cheek. Mary was always covered in whatever batter they were making. She did not hesitate, but went to the pantry and pulled out the apron that Lily usually wore on their rainy day activities and tossed it to her. Lily whispered 'I'm sorry' to Mary and the two were close all over again.

Chapter 5
Lily & the Magic Hug

Good night sweetie." Lily's mother tucked her in and kissed her on the forehead.

"Good night mommy, I love you!" Lily jumped up to meet her mother's arms. After a long embrace, Lily's mother returned her to the covers and tucked her in once again. As she was leaving the room, she gave Lily one last loving glance and waved.

"Nite-nite precious!" and then blew Lily a kiss.

As Lily lay in her warm bed thinking how awesome her family was, she drifted off to sleep. Dreaming about fluffy trees that looked like cotton candy. She dreamed she was walking through the fields and picking flowers when a dragon appeared and began to chase her. She ran with all her might up a hill and once she made it to the top, she fell. Before she hit the bottom, she woke up in a cold sweat. Lily was so frightened that she jumped up and ran to her parent's room. When she reached the door, she heard her mother screaming. It sounded as if someone was hurting her. She quickly pushed open the door to see what was happening. What she saw shocked her and she began to cry.

Her mother and father noticed that she was standing in the room. They both jumped as if they too were frightened.

Lily's mother asked, "Baby girl how long have you been standing there?" She slipped out of the covers and put on her robe. She then walked over to comfort Lily.

Lily felt so helpless. She was so shocked by what she saw, that she forgot all about the dragon dream. This was so strange to her. Why was her father hurting her mother? She thought they loved each other. Did this mean they were going to get a divorce? What was happening to her perfect family?

Lily asked in confusion, "What's going on?"

"Mommy and I were just sharing a special hug that's all." Her father went over to pick her up and hold her in his lap.

"Daddy you never hugged me like that. Why was mommy screaming? Were you hurting her?"

"No baby. You see sweetheart, there is a special hug that only husband and wives share. This special hug allows them to experience each other in a way that others cannot. When I was holding your mother, I was telling her I loved her in a different way than when I hold you. You and I share a father and daughter hug like this." He took Lily in his arms and squeezed her with all his might.

"Will she be alright?" Lily was still worried about her mother. "I don't want you two to get a divorce. Jeffrey's parent's got a divorce and he had to move away from school. I like it here. My best friend is here and I am just getting used to my room. Please don't divorce us daddy!" Lily began to cry.

"Pumpkin, there is no need for the water works." He began to laugh. "Your mother and I were just sharing love that's all. When you grow up and get a husband of your own you too will share the same love with him. You know that's how you got here."

Lily was more confused than ever. She thought of all the boys in her classroom. Each one of them was strange and yucky in his own way. She could never bring herself to touch them much less share a special hug. She expressed her displeasure outright.

"Yuck! That will never happen to me. Boys are gross!" Lily's father was secretly pleased because he wasn't ready for his little girl to be interested in boys just yet. He wanted to keep his little angel all to himself. He knew that one day this would change.

"Well kitten I'm happy to hear that, but please know it is important that you save that special part of yourself for the day you choose a husband. There is a lot of danger when you don't take care of yourself. You can get a very bad reputation or worse, you can get sick and die if you're not careful. The best way to avoid those types of dangers is to stay abstinent." Lily's father was not one to keep the truth from his baby girl.

"Daddy what does that mean?" Lily was curious to know what will keep her safe.

"Abstinence means that you will not share those special hugs with anyone until you are married to that special someone. I was lucky and found your mother and someday, a lucky man will find you."

"I will wait daddy. I will wait for that special man who will take care of me just like you, I promise." Lily was very proud of her father and knew that if her future husband was anything like him, she would be the lucky one.

Lily's daddy put his little girl back to bed and assured her that everything would be alright, and she drifted off to sleep knowing that it would be.

Chapter 6
Lily Remembers

It had been almost a year since Lily seen her hearse was long and black. It was the car that carried Papi's body to the cemetery or the place Me-maw and this was not a happy occasion. A cemetery is a place where the dead is buried. When everyone was in place, Father Rossi began interring or the ceremony that is usually held at grave sites.

He asked if there were any family or friends

who wanted to share any fond memories of the deceased. One of Lily's uncles began to tell a story of when they grew up in Mexico and they worked the fields. Someone else shared how caring and nurturing he had been. One of the neighbors told of how he and me-maw shared with them through a tough time. Before long, everyone was smiling and laughing at something that Papi said or did that touched their lives. However, none of this was funny to Lily. She saw nothing to smile or laugh about.

Lily's Papi had just died and she was not in a good mood at all. She felt so sad. She had never known sadness like this before. Even when her cat ran away, she did not feel this bad.

"Ashes to ashes; Dust to dust..." as Father Rossi spoke, he dropped petals from a chrysanthemum onto Papi's coffin. The reality that papa was gone set in. A few people shed some more tears as they began to walk away from the grave. Lily's held a rose in her hand that she tenderly placed on the shiny black box that would house her sweet grandfather forever. She wanted to give him one last hug or have him tickle her one last time, but he was gone.

Lily's mother took her hand and they walked up the hill back to the limousine that brought them there. As she climbed in the back, she saw them lower the coffin into the deep dark hole and she broke down into body quivering sobs. She felt an emptiness that nothing would ever fill.

Once they arrived at the old house she heard me-maw call to her, "Come in papoose!" Lily's grandmother was so happy to see her.

"Hello Me-maw how are you doing?" Lily looked around the house where she grew up. As she walked down the hallway to the kitchen, she noticed there were some familiar faces in the sitting room. She saw her aunt Priscilla and her cousins Gabriella and Manuel were there as well. Her uncle and his new wife also came to support Me-maw during this time of grieving.

Lily ran over to greet her aunt and uncle

when there was a knock at the door. Lily's grandmother excused herself and walked back to the front of the house. Lily's mother busied herself setting the dining room table buffet style. She had explained to Lily on the drive over that it was called a re-pass when everyone gathered after a funeral. It was done to comfort the family by bringing refreshments and remembering the deceased or the dead. This is usually a way for everyone to celebrate their part in the deceased person's life here on earth.

"Attention everyone...we will begin serving refreshments as soon as Father Rossi arrives." Lily's mother looked tired. She quickly returned to the kitchen. Lily decided to check on her. When she entered the kitchen she saw her mother leaning against the sink crying. Lily immediately ran over to comfort her. She hugged her mother with all her might. She was sad for herself, but it hurt her more to see her mother cry.

"Mommy do you miss Papi?" Lily wanted to take away her pain.

"Yes sweetheart. He was my father, but he was also my best friend. I could talk to Papi about anything. Whenever I was sad he always knew what to say to make me smile." She wiped her tears.

"Sounds like daddy and I. He is my best friend, and he always makes me laugh." Lily thought about how she would feel if she suddenly lost her daddy. She then understood why her mother was so sad.

"Hi Father Rossi. Welcome." Lily's Me-maw's voice interrupted her thoughts. Her mother took two tissues from the box on the counter and wiped her eyes. She then straightened out her apron and turned to Lily and smoothed out her hair.

"Are you ready to go sugar-pie?" She was trying so hard to look happy. Lily took her hand and led her towards the dining room.

When they entered the dining room, a few more of Papi's friends had arrived and there were also some more people from the church. Everyone stood around the table that was covered in food and held hands.

"Father Rossi, please offer a blessing for the food and fellowship." Me-maw was putting on the same brave front as Lily's mother. She held back her tears and bowed her head. Uncle Marcellas rubbed her shoulders to try and comfort her.

After the blessing was said, the feasting began. More people started to arrive bringing more food and offering their condolences or their support in this time of grieving. The party lasted for hours and we got the chance to see family and friends we haven't seen in years.

Finally the room began to clear and it was just the immediate family left. Papi had left specific instructions as to how he wanted his possessions divided up. This was called a will. He left it for Me-maw to read after his funeral. After she gave everyone their proper greetings, she read the will.

First, she gave all the beneficiaries their checks from the life insurance policy and then she divided up Papi's material possessions. Finally she finished with the properties in which my mother and father inherited some land and a car. Papi was a very generous man and he made sure he shared all that he had not just in life, but even in his death. After getting their allotments, the rest of the family started to leave. There was no one left but mommy and I to clean up.

"Me-maw are you going to miss Papi?" Lily wanted to know how she was feeling.

"Yes precious. He was my first love. We were married for 43 years and I will definitely miss him." She shed a few more tears.

"Where did you first meet him?" Lily's mother interrupted.

"We met at a fall festival. His family owned a stand at the local farmer's market and my parents were shopping for a pumpkin to carve for Halloween. Since it was Halloween and the jamboree was that night, all of the market people dressed up in costumes. My father picked the largest pumpkin he could find, but he couldn't lift it to put it on the back of his truck. The skinniest scarecrow I had ever seen rushed over to assist and that's when our eyes met. It was Jose. He gave me the sweetest smile. " Me-maw paused to smile. She told that story every Halloween. To most people it was a holiday of fear and dread but it was like Valentine's Day for me-maw and Papi.

"Well, that night at the jamboree he walked over and asked me to dance. I had never been to a dance before so I didn't know what I was doing. That didn't matter to him he just took my hand and showed me how to move to the music. He was such a gentleman. After that night we were inseparable." She smiled a little brighter.

"Will you ever marry again?" Lily was curious.

"Well sweetie, I have had the greatest love one could ever hope for with Papi. I don't know if I could ever find another so precious. I will keep my options open just in case though." We all laughed. It felt a little lighter in that kitchen watching as me-maw smiled and remembered the love of her life. Lily saw that this was the trick to getting over a death.

Always remember the happy times and the joy that person brought to your life.

"Me-maw, tell me some more! What was it like when you were dating?" Lily took a seat at the kitchen table and put her hands on her cheeks she was determined to cheer up her grandmother. It was working too, because with every question about Papi, Me-maw got happier. Remembering is like medicine it soothes the soul.

"Alright young lady, that's enough for today. Me-maw needs her rest." Lily's mother felt that she was being a burden, but Me-maw interrupted.

"Oh no, she's not being a burden at all. In fact, I have some old pictures of us when we first got married that I think you would love to see." Me-maw rushed into the living room and grabbed a photo album. She turned each page and had a story for every picture. As she and Lily strolled down memory lane, me-maw put some distance between herself and the pain of losing the best friend she ever had.

Printed in the United States
By Bookmasters